D1318517

Thomas the Tank Engine & Friends

A BRITT™ ALLCROFT COMPANY PRODUCTION

Based on The Railway Series by The Rev W Awdry
© Gullane (Thomas) LLC 2001

Visit the Thomas & Friends web site at www.thomasthetankengine.com

All rights reserved. Published by Scholastic Inc.
555 Broadway, New York, NY 10012

No part of this publication may be reproduced in whole or in part, or stored
in a retrieval system, or transmitted in any form or by any means,
electronic, mechanical, photocopying, recording, or otherwise, without
written permission of the publisher. For information regarding permission,
write to Scholastic Inc., Attention: Permissions Department,
555 Broadway, New York, NY 10012.
SCHOLASTIC and associated design is a trademark of Scholastic Inc.

ISBN 0-439-33839-5

12 11 10 9 8 7 6 5 4 3 2 1   1 2 3 4 5 6/0
Printed in the U.S.A.
First Scholastic printing, December 2001

HENRY and the Elephant

by
The REV. W. AWDRY

SCHOLASTIC INC.

New York   Toronto   London   Auckland   Sydney
Mexico City   New Delhi   Hong Kong   Buenos Aires

enry and Gordon were lonely when Thomas left the yard to run his branch line. They missed him very much.

They had more work to do. They couldn't wait in the shed till it was time, and find their coaches at the platform; they had to fetch them. They didn't like that.

Edward sometimes did odd jobs, and so did James, but James soon started grumbling, too. Sir Topham Hatt kindly gave Henry and Gordon new coats of paint (Henry chose green), but they still grumbled dreadfully.

"We get no rest, we get no rest," they complained as they clanked about the yard.

But the coaches only laughed. "You're lazy and slack, you're lazy and slack," they answered in their quiet, rude way.

But when a circus came to town, the engines forgot they were tired. They all wanted to shunt the special freight cars and coaches.

They were dreadfully jealous of James when Sir Topham Hatt told him to pull the train when the circus went away.

However, they soon forgot about the animals as they had plenty of work to do.

One morning, Henry was told to take some workmen to a tunnel that was blocked.

He grumbled away to find two freight cars to carry the workmen and their tools.

"Pushing freight cars! Pushing freight cars!" he muttered in a sulky sort of way.

They stopped outside the tunnel and tried to look through it, but it was quite dark; no daylight shone from the other end.

The workmen took their tools and went inside. Suddenly with a shout they all ran out looking frightened.

"We went to the block and started to dig, but it grunted and moved," they said.

"Rubbish," said the Foreman.

"It's not rubbish, it's big and alive; we're not going in there again."

"Right," said the Foreman, "I'll ride in a freight car, and Henry will push it out."

"*Wheeeesh*," said Henry unhappily. He hated tunnels (he had been shut up in one once) but this was worse; something big and alive was inside.

"*Peep peep peep pip pip pee—eep!*" he whistled, "I don't want to go in!"

"Neither do I," said his Driver, "but we must clear the line."

"Oh, dear! Oh, dear!" puffed Henry as they slowly advanced into the darkness.

BUMP——!!!!

Henry's Driver shut off steam at once.

"Help! Help! We're going back," wailed Henry, and slowly moving out into the daylight came first Henry, then the freight cars, and last of all, pushing hard and rather cross, came a large elephant.

"Well, I never!" said the Foreman. "It's an elephant from the circus."

Henry's Driver put on his brakes, and a man ran to telephone for the keeper.

The elephant stopped pushing and came toward them. They gave him some sandwiches and cake, so he forgot he was cross and remembered he was hungry. He drank three buckets of water without stopping and was just going to drink another when Henry let off steam.

The elephant jumped, and "*hoo——oosh*," he squirted the water all over Henry by mistake.

Poor Henry!

When the keeper came, the workmen rode home happily in the freight cars laughing at their adventure, but Henry was very cross.

"An elephant pushed me! An elephant hooshed me!" he hissed.

He was sulky all day, and his coaches had an uncomfortable time.

In the shed, he told Gordon and James about the elephant, and I am sorry to say that instead of laughing and telling him not to be silly, they looked sad and said, "You poor engine, you have been badly treated."

Now flip the book over to start another Thomas & Friends adventure.

Workmen made Henry a temporary coupling. They rejoined him to his tender, and then the Driver and Fireman lit a new fire and drove him gently home.

Edward, who had of course seen everything, told the others. They were careful what they talked about that night.

As for Henry, he was touchy on the subject of fires for some time afterward. But James was quick to notice that from then on Henry stopped making rude remarks about the color of fire engines.

Now flip the book over to start another Thomas & Friends adventure.

While the Fireman dealt with the fire, the Driver went back to tell the Signalman what had happened. When he returned, he found Henry completely hidden in a huge cloud of black smoke, which billowed from beneath his cab.

The Fireman emerged, choking. "Henry's fire set the sleepers alight," he spluttered. "You stay here—I'm going to phone the fire brigade."

The Driver eased Henry clear of the blaze, and then Edward came to take his train on to the next station. Henry felt most uncomfortable.

Henry stopped as soon as he could. The automatic brake halted his tender and the train some distance behind.

"We must drop Henry's fire," said the Driver urgently. "It will be dangerous to let him boil dry now that we can't get more water from the tender."

The Fireman agreed.

"Sorry, old boy," he said to Henry. "Just when we'd got going nicely, too. But if you hadn't banged about so much you wouldn't have broken your tender coupling."

No one noticed the rattle from beneath Henry's footplate as he snorted away, and soon the train was running well.

"Hurry, hurry, hurry," puffed Henry. Faster and faster they went. At last, Henry began to feel better.

Suddenly he heard a crack from below his cab.

"Look out!" shouted the Driver. He applied the brakes while the Fireman scrambled forward to the footplate. He was just in time. Both men watched in horror as a widening gap opened between Henry and his tender.

Henry was still cross the next morning.

"What can be wrong? What can be wrong?" wondered the coaches anxiously as Henry pulled noisily away from the big station.

"Do come along, do come along," Henry snorted impatiently.

They had a fast run, but it didn't improve Henry's temper. He bumped the coaches when they reached the end of the line, and again when he backed up to them for the return journey. He simmered angrily while the Fireman fastened the coupling.

"I like my green, too," agreed Henry. "I'd hate to be red like James. People would think I was a fire engine."

"At least people can see me coming," retorted James. "I don't disappear into the background like some engines I could mention. If it wasn't for the noise, you'd need a yellow and black front like Mavis."

Henry's protests were drowned in the laughter of the other engines, and he went to sleep wondering how to pay James back.

" 'Flying Scotsman' and my brothers were all green," explained Gordon one night in the shed. "It was all very well in its way, but now I prefer my blue. It makes me different, you see, and that's very suitable for an important engine like me."

"The engines on oor auld line used to be blue," remembered Donald, "but nae sae dark as we are. Dougie and me never were though—we had to be black, sae blue makes a nice change."

FIRE ENGINE

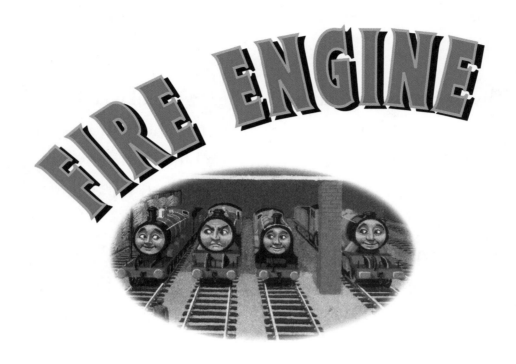

by
The REV. W. AWDRY

SCHOLASTIC INC.

New York   Toronto   London   Auckland   Sydney
Mexico City   New Delhi   Hong Kong   Buenos Aires

Thomas the Tank Engine & Friends

A BRITT ALLCROFT COMPANY PRODUCTION

Based on The Railway Series by The Rev W Awdry
© Gullane (Thomas) LLC 2001

Visit the Thomas & Friends web site at www.thomasthetankengine.com

All rights reserved. Published by Scholastic Inc.
555 Broadway, New York, NY 10012

No part of this publication may be reproduced in whole or in part, or stored
in a retrieval system, or transmitted in any form or by any means,
electronic, mechanical, photocopying, recording, or otherwise, without
written permission of the publisher. For information regarding permission,
write to Scholastic Inc., Attention: Permissions Department,
555 Broadway, New York, NY 10012.
SCHOLASTIC and associated design is a trademark of Scholastic Inc.

ISBN 0-439-33839-5

12 11 10 9 8 7 6 5 4 3 2 1   1 2 3 4 5 6/0
Printed in the U.S.A.
First Scholastic printing, December 2001

FIRE ENGINE